FOOTMAN   USHER   FLOOR
MANAGER   CHIEF
USHER

The SATURDAY KID

The SATURDAY

Leo tried to explain, but the usher grabbed his collar and dragged him up the aisle. Out on the street, Leo could only think of getting even with Morty, who always spoiled things. Maybe when he was grown up he would be a G-man, and Morty would be a criminal. Leo would round up Morty and his gang and . . .

Just at that moment, Leo saw his mother on her way home from work. On Saturdays she came home early and cooked something special for dinner. Leo helped carry the groceries up the four flights of stairs to their apartment where his dog, Pal, was waiting.

That evening after dinner, Leo took out his violin and began to practice *Estrellita* (Little Star). Once he started to play, he forgot all about Morty.

After school on Thursdays he would hurry off to his violin lesson.
Mr. Kleinberg, his teacher, lived way downtown near Union Square.
Leo would rush off to the wonderful Third Avenue elevated train
that ran high above the street. It ran right next to apartment win-
dows. Looking into people's rooms was just like watching a movie,
Leo thought.

One Thursday, Leo met his teacher even further downtown than usual, at City Hall. He had been chosen to represent his school at the Mayor's Young Musicians Concert. It was an important event, with children there from many different schools. Leo played *Estrellita* without a single mistake. Afterwards, the Mayor shook hands with all the young performers. He told Leo he was "a mighty fine fiddler." What's more, the Mayor said it right in front of a newsreel camera.

The next day, Leo waited till after school to tell his friends about the concert. When he got to the part about shaking hands with the Mayor, Morty interrupted. "You're full of baloney," he snarled. Leo knew Morty was just trying to pick a fight, so he turned his back and started home. "What a bully!" he thought. Morty was like the big show-off in the movie *Captain Blood*. Someday Leo would get his revenge like the daring buccaneer on the pirate ship and . . .

When Leo got home, Pal was waiting for him with a wagging tail and a happy bark. He took Pal for a walk, and afterwards they wrestled on the easy chair for a while. Leo told Pal about Morty, and Pal gave a sympathetic wag. Then Pal went to sleep, and Leo brought out his violin.

On Monday night Leo was practicing a new piece when Mr. Kleinberg telephoned to say he could not see Leo on Thursday that week, and could he come Saturday afternoon instead? Leo didn't want to miss Saturday at the movies, but he also didn't want to disappoint Mr. Kleinberg or his mother. He guessed his friends could tell him how Dick Tracy escaped this time. So he said, "Sure."

On Saturday Leo walked past the Luxor to the Third Avenue El. The main movie was about World War I pilots who wore exactly the same kind of helmet Leo was wearing. Morty and some other boys were waiting for the theater to open. Leo walked straight ahead, but Morty spotted him. "Where ya goin', big shot?" he shouted. "Gonna play for the President?"

As Leo walked on towards the station, all he could think of was
how much he hated Morty. Why did Morty always pick on him? he
wondered. Then the train came, and Leo hopped on the first car so
he could look out the front window. The train traveled fast and high
above the street. To Leo, it was just like an airplane. In his helmet
and goggles he felt like a World War I pilot, a flying ace in *Dawn
Patrol*. Suddenly, out of the clouds came an enemy plane and . . .

Leo came down to earth just as the train arrived at his station, and he barely managed to squeeze out the door before it closed.

He hurried across Union Square Park, which was crowded with people making speeches. Leo would have liked to stop, but he couldn't be late for his lesson.

Mr. Kleinberg's apartment was small and jammed full of books, magazines, and phonograph records. Leo tried out some new music, but the best part of the lesson was when he and his teacher played a duet together. At the end of the hour Leo handed him the two dollars his mother always put in an envelope. This time Mr. Kleinberg surprised him by suggesting they go to the Automat for a hot chocolate. "Saturdays are for having fun," he said.

At the Automat Mr. Kleinberg gave Leo six nickels—enough to buy hot chocolate and a piece of pie. After studying the rows and rows of pies, Leo dropped four nickels in the slot next to the cherry pie, opened the door, and took out the plate. With the other two nickels he got hot chocolate. While they ate, Leo described how Morty wouldn't believe he had played before the Mayor. "Well," said Mr. Kleinberg, "sometimes people get angry at other people who do things they can't do."

It wasn't yet dark when Leo got home, so he was surprised to see the table already set for dinner. "Are we going somewhere?" he asked.

"Well, if you're not too tired," his mother said with a smile, "I thought we'd eat and then go to the Paradise to see a movie."

Leo couldn't believe his ears. Loew's Paradise! His favorite theater—many times bigger than the Luxor and much more beautiful. At the Paradise, the ushers wore gold-braided uniforms. He'd never be too tired to go there!

He and his mother entered the glittering lobby and headed for the balcony. Leo wanted to be close to the theater's famous ceiling of twinkling stars and floating clouds. As they started up the elegant staircase with its thick red carpeting, Leo heard a familiar voice. Turning, he saw Morty and his parents. Leo was horrified. What if the usher seated them next to his mother and him?

That was exactly
what happened. But with his
parents present, Morty behaved. The house
lights dimmed and the newsreel came
on. It wasn't very interesting — a scene of
soldiers marching, followed by a football game.
Then suddenly the camera moved to City Hall,
and Leo heard his mother gasp, "Leo, look!
That's you!" There on the giant screen were
the young musicians, Leo playing the violin,
Leo shaking hands with the Mayor, and a
close-up of them both. Leo's face was the size
of a three-story building!

After the newsreel ended, Leo had a hard time concentrating on the movie that followed. So did his mother. At last the lights came on, and Morty's parents turned to congratulate Leo and his mother on his success. They all walked out together. Morty's father told Leo to "keep up the good work," and his mother told Leo's mother how much she wished she had a son who could play the violin. Morty didn't say anything at all. Leo almost felt sorry for him.

Leo's mother had one more surprise for him. "Becoming a movie star calls for a celebration," she said, "and that looks like the perfect place for it." She pointed to Krum's Ice Cream Parlor across the street.

They sat at the counter and Leo ordered a hot fudge sundae. "I still can't believe it," he said. "I can't believe I was on the screen at the Paradise with the Mayor shaking my hand!"

On the bus ride home, Leo and his mother kept on smiling. People began to look at them strangely. Leo's smile widened when he realized that some of them must have seen the newsreel and recognized him. He wondered what Morty would say when they met in the schoolyard on Monday. Somehow, Leo was pretty certain that his troubles with Morty were over.

Nobody would mess with the Saturday kid!

WS ABRIL 3 2001

THE STAFF AT

ELEVATOR
OPERATOR

PAGE BOY

DOORMAN

STREETMAN